Frank popped another ephedrine tab, chased it with cold coffee, heard the opening strains of O Come All Ye Faithful, and punched it off. Had to be careful now to keep it on all-talk, carols becoming harder and harder to steer clear of. He nursed the rig back up to speed. Couple more days...

This time it broke loose for real.

Bethany

"The sheer beauty and strength of Barre's writing gives a glow of redemption that is extremely rare in any kind of fiction."

— DICK ADLER

Chicago Tribune

"There is a spooky polish rubbed over all of this, onto every surface until it shines. Barre knows what he is doing and this story shows it. Edgar [Allen Poe] would be proud because it ripples with the muscle of less being more."

— MICHAEL CONNELLY

best-selling author of *Lost Light*

"Although known as a writer of outstanding detective novels, Richard Barre has written a suspense story of extraordinary poignancy that will keep readers at the edge of their seats as they dry their eyes."

— OTTO PENZLER

The Mysterious Bookshop, New York

"Richard Barre touches the soul. He is simply one of the best."

— HARLAN COBEN

best-selling author of *No Second Chance*

Other Books by Richard Barre

The Innocents
Bearing Secrets
The Ghosts of Morning
Blackheart Highway
The Star
Burning Moon

Bethany

Richard Barre

Foreword by Robert Crais

CAPRA PRESS
MEMORABLE BOOKS SINCE 1969
SANTA BARBARA

A Robert Bason Book
Published by Capra Press
815 De La Vina Street
Santa Barbara, CA 93101
www.caprapress.com

Cover and book design by Frank Goad

Library of Congress Cataloging-in-Publication Data

Barre, Richard.
Bethany / by Richard Barre.
p. cm.
ISBN 1-59266-038-X (trade hardcover)
ISBN 1-59266-039-8 (numbered hardcover)
ISBN 1-59266-040-1 (lettered hardcover)
1. Truck drivers—Fiction.
2. Blizzards—Fiction.
3. Widowers—Fiction.
I. Title.
PS3552.A73253B48 2003
813'.54—dc21
2003005415

Edition: 10 9 8 7 6 5 4 3 2 1
First Edition

Second in the Series

FOREWORD

ROBERT CRAIS

Flip a switch, and life snaps into focus. The switch could be anything: a cancer scare, the way light catches in the spring-green leaves, those first crispy wrinkles that appear around your eyes, or a traffic accident in the middle of nowhere late on a frozen night.

Flip a switch, and suddenly the review of a life can be reduced to chilling absolutes: good or hopeless, rich or wasted, worthy or lost. No one judges us more harshly than we judge ourselves, and we are never more merciless with these self-assessments than when we are weak. In these times we see ourselves in the darkest light, without middle ground, and the reviews with which we damn ourselves can contain descriptives such as "failure" and "loser."

The switch is flipped, and we can spiral into hopelessness, seeing only our losses but never our gains.

But by the flip of that same switch…maybe we have a chance to see everything that is good in us and, in that moment, have one final chance at redemption.

No one has done this better in any form than Rod Serling. I loved that show – Rod Serling's *The Twilight Zone* – where week after week, Serling offered up stylish, heart-breaking examinations of traveling salesmen, bookish nerds, retirement-home foundlings, and other lost souls staring down the barrels of their own lost lives. Serling delivered these dramas with poignancy and insight, and the poetry of a talent who sensed, innately, that everyone carries within themselves a core of "good" worth saving.

Bethany is such a story.

Richard Barre shows the same depth and humanity that illuminated Serling's work by reminding us – as we question ourselves in bleak moments – of the questions we often forget to ask: Are the switches flipped by chance or design? Are we being given a curse or a gift? A chance not to see weakness, but an opportunity to affirm strength? And if a switch has indeed been switched...by whom?

ROBERT CRAIS

April 2003

Bethany

F

rank Shane never saw the ice.

He was making good time, no problem there: Oregon border and Mount Shasta back of him, eighty miles to Lakehead and the dam, load of Christmas trees from up near the Idaho border behaving itself behind him.

So far, so good.

Mind over matter.

Old growth closed in around a whitened cut in the hill, retreated behind a fringe of rock-crush, then dropped off to white before shadowing up the other side. Even in storm it was nice country: clean and wooded *before* descending to the farms and valley sprawl, Big-Macs, off-brand self-serves and ag-supply billboards. Which still beat by miles where he was living after having to sell the house.

Spokane…

Downtown Spokane…

His thoughts turned to the snow swirling in his low-beams, wondering if he'd be able to outrun it. Snowing all the way to Redding from the jawbone he'd heard on the two-way gone quiet a bit ago, nothing he much missed, guys mostly talking about their black-book entries.

All he needed.

A swirl closed in, broke apart in the beams, then a longer one that eased in a lee before heavying up again. Not the most promising of conditions, maybe, but all right with a break or two.

Then the feeling.

Ice, no question: black ice, feathery lightness in the steering, a sense of drifting into the curve instead of adhering to it. Scary as a mother, with 65,000 lbs. of trailer set to follow its own law of physics.

But the tires caught and he breathed again, eased up on the 560 horses, let the big-rig slip back under forty despite the deadline he was fighting. No sleep in the last twenty-two hours, none likely in the next fourteen.

L.A. needing its freaking Christmas trees.

Not that it wasn't good money, it was. All the more, it would help make a dent in his spiraling black-hole nightmare, denizens of which included doctors, anesthesiologists, radiologists – some who'd even managed to sound involved while Ginny lay in there waiting for what never came, a chance.

Which wasn't being fair, but what was…life?

Right.

Frank reached up to his visor and touched the photograph, his favorite of her: sun backlighting her hair, the one where she'd suddenly felt the surf backwashing her feet and laughed at the sensation. The one he'd taken during their trip to the Yucatan.

BL…before the lump.

Frank blinked, threw his attention back to the road. No mystery about where the ice had come from; snowmelt from earlier cascading down the embankment had set up hard and invisible with the plummeting temperature. This before the snow had begun in earnest to clear I-5 of its remaining traffic, nobody else but him fool enough to strap it on in this weather.

The road ghost, he thought, good CB handle.

Frank popped another ephedrine tab, chased it with cold coffee, heard the opening strains of *O Come All Ye Faithful* and punched it off. Had to be careful now to keep it on all-talk, carols becoming harder and harder to steer clear of. He nursed the rig back up to speed. Couple more days…

This time it broke loose for real.

Instantly he backed off, fought the urge to hit the Jake-brake, slow the rig by what amounted to compression – like the brake pedal, a sure way to lock up on ice. Instead he turned toward the skid and hung on, about all he could do, that and hope for a soft hillside. Pray, maybe.

Real future there, alright.

Permanent squelch.

Besides, the future was now. It was like watching another rig in the rearview attempting to pass, only it was his own load, long as a five-story building was tall, jackknifing at the hitch. He was conscious of median and berm beyond the Peterbuilt's nose, slopeoff leading to the river – where the thing that once was a 74-foot tractor-trailer under his control was heading in slow motion, or what seemed like it.

Richard Barre

He heard the rig groaning, roadside reflectors snapping off, ice crunching and buckling, buckshot gravel under tires headed sideways. Then the trailer was off the shoulder, tail leading the dog. Rolling and grinding and jolting its way down the slope, an eternity of seconds until the rig tore into firs and pines and cottonwoods, plowing up forest and coming to rest upside down. Close enough for Frank to hear the roar of rapids through the smashed windshield.

Just before he went out.

Freezing cold, the sound of wind adding to the rush of water.

Frank opened his eyes, slowly took inventory: Beyond a lump behind his ear, tacky blood in his hair and on his face, nothing felt broken. Then he moved his knee and nearly passed out.

Shit…

Shit, shit, shit.

He appraised it gingerly: nothing crunched and no bones protruding – sprained, likely, or badly bruised. In the faint orange light of the dash, he was able to find his flashlight and scan for damage. The cab looked as if it were a couple of feet shorter, no glass left in any of the windows, this topsy-turvy world. Snow gleamed back at him where it had drifted inside. Luckily, there was no smell of fuel; the tanks hadn't ruptured.

Frank reached for and keyed off the ignition, set the flash down, unharnessed himself, eased into a position where he could reach the CB. Smashed, of course – from the red paint on it, by the fire extinguisher now lying against the dome light.

Anything else in your bag of tricks?

Hell, why stop there?

He checked his watch: 9:07 – he'd been out more than thirty minutes. He beamed on the outside thermometer, saw intact dial showing fourteen degrees. Behind him in the mirror, the sleeper cab resembled a Coors can crushed during one of his benders, a fat-trunked pine emerging on either side of the crease. No salvaging anything in there.

Frank reached out what remained of his side window, felt jagged splinters and rough bark. He tried the passenger side and this time punched through, cleared an opening in the snow and eased his banged-up knee out, then head and shoulders. Putting the weight on his right leg, he got to his feet, smelled Christmas trees super strong, and made out his load, dead lumps scattered to the limits of his vision.

Bye-bye payday; hello repo man.

Better if he hadn't come to.

Snowflakes swirled around him, mocked him; the river sounded as if he were standing right in it. Sure enough, his beam picked out brown water moving fast and high, angry through a break in some branches, impressive some other time. As to now, he was beginning to lose feeling in his fingers he was so cold.

He looked back at the Coors can, thought about his parka inside and dismissed it. Might as well be on the moon for all the good it was to him now, cutoff sweatshirt over a tee his sole protection. *Freezing.* He set the flash on a rock, waved his arms to get some feeling back, started sizing up where he stood – beyond his sole asset lying wheels up.

Belly up was more like it.

He shone the light up toward the highway and got only snow; straining to hear, he heard only wind. This late, storm warnings coming all day, they'd have closed the road to traffic, maybe open tomorrow if it let up. Nothing to indicate that from the reports and what he was seeing.

Stay in the cab he'd be ice by morning, assuming anybody could find him under a dump of this magnitude, any sign of his going off where he did long since erased. Slip and slide back up the slope? More like climbing Everest on one leg, and for what – freeze up there, freeze down here. *God, it was cold.* Still, he was considering dragging himself up, taking his chances on a stray smokey or plow, when he cast a glance over his shoulder and saw the light.

Gone in the time it took to blink.

Which figured, of course – the bump on the head. To be certain, Frank turned off his flash and still saw nothing. Then the wind blew a branch out of his line of sight, and there it was again. Enough at least to cancel further debate.

Favoring his knee, Frank started along the river's edge. Footing was treacherous, the snow about two feet deep but powdery, some good in that. The light seemed across the river and up a rise, back from the bank – hard to tell with the snow in his face, eyes watering from the wind. He'd gone about a half mile by his calculation and was about to buy into the irony of freezing ten yards across a river from apparent safety, when he

Richard Barre

saw the bridge.

Not exactly a bridge, as he drew closer, more suspension apparatus for a pipe running across. But the thing had hand cables, and going slowly he was able to hobble over the torrent, the wind more than once making him think he was going in and how quickly it went to hell on you.

Like with Ginny.

Nineteen years together and *wham* – nothing he could do for her, a dark universe light years distant. Surely not from where he'd *been*, out on the road most of that time, trying to keep them afloat as she drifted away beyond his reach.

Only his life.

Across the river now, he swept the flash around, caught the outline of a trail through weighted trees plopping white. At least the incline was gentle. Gritting for it, taking it slow, Frank kept on until he reached the light, breath burning in his chest and his knee resembling a peg leg, each jolt to it reminding him it wasn't.

The light he'd seen was fixed to the side of an A-frame shed: locked tight, no windows to break, no prospects for shelter. Except maybe on the road winding past it, assuming that was what lay under the drifting white blanket. The one that led to glowing windows about a hundred yards up.

Hands so numb he could barely grip the flash, breath ragged with cold and exertion, Frank lurched the rest of the way – up onto a short porch where he collapsed against the half-log exterior.

The splash of light as the door was opened and someone stepped out was as beautiful as he'd ever seen.

She was bent over him, rubbing his hands and arms, when he jerked awake, saw light brown hair swept upward and back, a face about his age, forty-three. Warm hazel eyes, solid features, cheeks without make-up and flushed with color. Probably from the effort of having to drag him inside, he figured, to where he was propped against a leatherette booth.

"Welcome back," she said.

Long denim skirt, blue-checked blouse inside a navy wool sweater vest. Tallish as she stood back from him, the air smelling of soup and baked things.

"Where are we?" he asked. Easing back the heavy blanket she'd put around his shoulders, the chill in him

Richard Barre

more or less gone.

"No place much," she said. "Leastwise not anymore, it isn't. Bethany, if you need a name. Nearest town's a good fifteen miles."

She had a voice that fit her, warm with a little crack in it. He glanced over her shoulder.

"This a restaurant?"

"Just my old café, but thanks for the compliment. Least you're not out there."

He leaned against the booth, everything rushing in on him.

"You all right?" Concern in her eyes matching her tone.

"Oh yeah. One good deal after another."

She braced and lent him an arm, and he managed to get up, the knee stiff and aching, a feeling like burn on his hands. He stood, felt dizzy, eased down inside the booth.

"Stay right there," she ordered.

He watched her step behind stools and a counter, fill a ceramic mug, lace it from a brandy bottle underneath. His eyes left her to take in the room: comfortably tidy, half-dozen booths like the one he was sitting in. Chintz curtains and brown oilcloth, rectangular opening through to the kitchen, a thing to put up orders for the cook. Near the register a view container, its glass shelves stacked with pies in various stages of consumption.

She wedged a slab onto a plate, brought it to him with the coffee and brandy, slid in across from him. "Figured you might know what to do with this," she said. "And my name's Claire." Extending a hand he took, noting its warmth and grip.

"Frank." He tried the pie, realized how hungry he was, how good it tasted, some kind of berry. "Thanks," he said after finishing, "What do I owe you?" Sounding inadequate, but wanting to offer.

"Forget it. Looks like you took quite a shot there."

He followed her eyes, touched the spot behind his ear, saw the melting snow was reconstituting the blood. He took the cloth she'd been using and dabbed at it. "Nothing much. Just a bump."

"Mind if I ask why you're here? I mean, at least I've got an excuse."

Grinding metal, snow vortexing in the headlights, the feeling of being worked over with a crowbar.

"My truck hit some ice and went off the highway."

"Lord. You were out driving in this?"

He focused back, swallowed the last of the coffee. "Not much choice in the matter."

She refilled it, this time without the brandy. "Unless you're in jail, it seems to me you always have a choice. Or am I missing something?"

"Not unless you're partial to pulling the wings off flies."

She looked puzzled, the way Ginny had after they'd adjusted her painkillers. Something twinged inside him and let go. "It's a long story, nothing I'm gonna bore you with. Would you have a phone?"

She shook her head. "The lines are down. Only reason we have power now is the generator my husband put in for such as this."

Frank scanned the kitchen, saw no movement, no white apron emerging from a walk-in or shaking snow off. "And would your husband be around?"

"Oh no, he died years ago. It's just us."

"Us..." Frank said.

"Right." Extending a thumb. "You, me, and *her*."

The girl Claire had gestured to lay on a bunk in a living

area off the kitchen. Tiny little thing, her face set in a grimace. Frank could see her swollen abdomen under the blanket lying across her. Limp brown hair, fine-featured face beaded with perspiration.

Her blue eyes left a spot on the ceiling, met his as Claire bathed her face with a damp towel, soothed her with something he couldn't hear. He saw a smile break before she moaned softly and closed her eyes.

He eased back from the alcove, waited for Claire to emerge. On reflex, he tried the phone, heard nothing and put the receiver back.

"She's a runaway off one of the ranches," Claire said, rinsing out the towel. "Came in about the time the phone quit."

"Runaway from what?" Frank asked because it seemed called for.

"From the uncle who did it. Nothing like a ten-mile walk to induce labor."

Great. "How old is she?"

"Fourteen, if she's telling the truth." She squeezed out the towel, dropped it into a pot over a gas flame. "You remember being that age? I hadn't even been kissed yet."

Frank looked at her more closely, saw younger than

he'd first imagined, mid-to-late thirties, not bad look-ing in a country sort of way. "Fourteen's when I started driving truck, helping out my dad, for all the good it's done." He gestured toward the alcove. "You going to try and get her to a hospital or something?"

"In those drifts? I don't think so." She looked at him. "What..."

He realized he'd been staring. "Just curious. You told her something that seemed to make her feel better. About me?"

"You could say that."

Something in her expression. "Mind if I ask what?"

Pause, the hint of a smile. "The girl's scared to death her baby won't live unless a doctor's present. First words out of her after I got her defrosted." His look must have said it, because she didn't wait for a response, adding, "All you have to do is follow instructions."

"Instructions? What instructions?" The chill sud-denly back. "Lady, this is not my problem."

"I'm afraid it is, actually. I told her it was a miracle, a doctor coming here out of that storm."

"*You told her – ?*"

"Please, not so loud. She'll hear you."

"*I don't believe this.*"

"It might be better if you tried."

Holy Flaming Moses. "Lady – Claire – if I'm a doctor, you're the Virgin Mary."

They'd finished the food Claire made. At her insistence, Frank had gone in to try to reassure the girl, act like he knew what he was doing, still ticked at being maneuvered. To his surprise, he hadn't had to say much, just hold her hand until some contractions passed. Back in the dining room, he asked Claire if she had any cigarettes, suddenly feeling the need.

"I wouldn't," she said. "Sorry."

"I'll bet."

"Do you mind? I've midwifed babies. It's going to be fine. Someone may even come by then."

Frank glanced at the windows, the whirl of falling snow, and felt a sensation like the floor dropping out. He forced himself to take a breath, stop pacing, slump in a dining chair.

A moment passed. She said, "Things aren't very good right now, are they? I mean besides your accident."

"Excuse me?"

"Forgive me for being nosy, but I'm getting a feeling it's your wife. You're separated, or she's sick or something."

"I have no idea what you're talking about." As if his voice had atrophied.

"Nothing to be afraid of. Ever since I was a girl, I've had this gift of sight, seeing into people. I've also lost a spouse, remember? It's written all over you."

He let out a breath, ached for a smoke. Too hot in here, too cold to go back outside. *Shit.*

"How long has it been?"

"Lady, with all due respect, that's none of your business."

"Claire. And believe me, it helps."

"*Bullshit, it helps.* Nothing helps."

He watched her drop her eyes to her hands: weathered skin and red knuckles, work and more work. *Perfect.* "Six months and a couple of days. Tomorrow would have been her birthday, so you'll pardon me if – "

"I'm sorry," she said. "Truly."

"Me, too. Helluva day, is all."

She hooked a cloth out of the pot, dipped it in one with cooled water, swirled it around. "What are you going to do about your truck?"

Not liking this direction much better, he said, "Put

it this way, I won't be paying off any medical bills for a while. Let alone making truck payments."

She waited, as if knowing more was coming.

Okay, Lady – you want it, you can have it. "Do you have any idea how it feels losing everything? Wishing you'd died too?"

"I think so."

"Yeah, well – sorry to rain on your parade, but I'm not big on miracles right now."

"You're already a miracle to that girl. Did you see how she looked at you?"

"Look – *Claire* – I'm grateful for your help. I've also been called a lot of things, but none so far off the mark."

She sipped coffee.

Hazel eyes regarded him over the lip of her mug.

"So – what's your sign?" he said after Claire had introduced the girl as Rachel, him to her as *Dr.* Shane, Claire giving him a look like, *That's the best you can do?* Frank trying without luck to recall doctor movies and TV shows he'd seen, stethoscopes about it. The aspirin

Claire had given him calming the knee some at least.

"I'm not sure," Rachel said in her girl voice, tightening as a spasm hit and passed. "My birthday is February 23rd."

"Pisces," he said. "Same sign as mine."

Her eyes widened. "That's a good omen, don't you think?"

"I suppose. Have you picked a name for it?"

"Not yet. But I just know it's a boy. Claire agreed with me."

Claire agreed.

"That's nice."

"No, it's – "

With that the power went out.

Dead silence, then Rachel moaning, reaching out for him, Frank taking her hand, feeling the fear in her grip. Claire saying, "Nothing to worry about, just the generator acting up. I've fixed it before."

With his free hand, Frank found his lighter and flicked it on, saw Claire getting a candle from a drawer she'd felt her way to. He leaned the lighter into the wick, watched it flame. Moments later they had a dozen going.

"See," she said, "we don't even need it. You okay, Hon?"

Rachel managed a nod.

"Just like the Boy Scouts," Frank said. "Be prepared?"

"Doctor," Claire said. "Can I have a word with you?"

"I suppose. If Rachel doesn't mind." Trying at least to measure his sarcasm.

They moved out into the dining room.

"I don't like it," Claire said quietly. "It doesn't feel right."

"Well, if you're looking for a second opinion, don't." Shaking out another ephedrine and chasing it with water.

"It's not dilating properly."

"What's not?"

"I can make out the head, but it's not moving down."

"Can't blame it much. Probably terrified."

She ignored the crack.

"All right," he filled in. "What?"

"If things don't improve, we'll have to go in. You've heard of caesarean section?"

Icewater, a look to see she was serious, no sign of not. "Just where does *we* come into this?"

"What I meant was, we could lose them both."

Frank rubbed eyes that felt splashed with road salt, thought about Rachel in there, about Ginny, all of it. *Son of a bitch.*

"He's at it again, isn't he?" Almost to himself.

She glanced up. "Who are you talking about?"

"Who do you think I'm talking about? That is, assuming you're a believer."

There was a pause. "I see. Which I take it you aren't?"

"Let's just say he doesn't fool me anymore."

"And why would you say that?"

"You mean apart from the swell examples in my life?"

She was silent. Taking it for retreat and just on general principle, he added, "Don't get out much, huh? Look around – that girl in there for starters."

"What about her?"

"You sure you want to go there?"

"I don't understand the – "

"Oh, I think you do. See, I know him by his work. Firsthand. And all the words and all the prayers in the world don't make up for one Ginny Shane. That clear enough?"

"You're angry."

"Lady, you have no idea."

She wrung out the cloths, set them in a row. "I might. I was that way when I lost Sewell. I'm sorry, my husband."

"Okay, I'll bite." His wave having crashed and receded somewhat. "What happened to Sewell?"

"My husband drowned."

"And that's all you're going to say?"

"Years ago, during a flood we had. The bridge was out and I was trying to get across to him. He died trying to save me."

Frank nodded. "Sounds like the big guy, all right. Real sense of humor."

"I came to terms with it."

"Congratulations."

She paused, unsure how far to take it. Then, "Tell me. What would your wife say about using her like this?"

His turn to hesitate. "I'm alive, she isn't. His call."

"Did you ever consider it might be part of something bigger than you?"

"Ah, the old standby: I don't get it. At least *that* you got right." Sick of it, the pain it brought, but at the same time grounded by the simple act of confronting another human being, the heat of friction after so much

Richard Barre

empty cold.

God, was he really that needy?

She walked to the window, rubbed a spot in the condensation, looked out at the snow. "That said, are you just going to *let* him get away with it?"

"What's that mean?"

"Rachel's eaten nothing to speak of in two days. She's already hemorrhaged. She's weak, which means the baby's weak. Even with both of us, they could die. Now, are you going to *let* him get away with that?"

Frank chewed on it. "Foul up his plan is what you're saying."

"Something like that."

Deep breath. "Lady, I know one thing: I'm too beat to keep this up for long." Not letting on that her idea wasn't lost on him, just that he hadn't thought of it in those terms.

"Does that mean yes or no?"

"*Jesus*," he said. "Why here?"

Two a.m., the cafe's air dense from steam off the boiling water, Claire still working on Rachel, nothing he could see, thankfully. Rachel's moans had turned to screams, like something out of a horror film. Even Ginny's hadn't been this bad.

"*GOD,*" Rachel screamed. "*GOD OH GOD OH GOD OH GOD OH GOD…*"

Nice work, Frank thought, hope you're proud of yourself. He wiped her face with an already damp towel. "Come on Rachel, you're doing fine. Just a little longer."

Frank Shane, M.D. and headcase.

"Doctor," Claire said, tense, but placid by comparison. "I need you down here."

"Say again?"

"I believe you heard me."

"Are you out of your mind?" Lowering his voice.

No response.

"I said – "

"Now, doctor."

"*GOD,*" Rachel screamed.

"RIGHT NOW."

Taking short breaths, Frank went.

Richard Barre

Between two and four, they worked to exploit even the slightest movement, to keep Rachel's efforts in sync — increasingly hard with the contractions she was experiencing — Frank running cloths back and forth from the stove, careful not to skid on the trail of drips. Until Claire said, "See how I have my hands positioned?"

"So?" Well past squeamish by now.

"The cord is prolapsed — pinched in there. Unless we make room for it, the baby gets no blood or oxygen. That's what I've been doing the last two hours. But my hands are cramping. I need you to spell me."

Chill again, despite how far he'd come.

"Did you hear me, Doctor?"

"Yes," Hearing her, but not.

"Frank, I'm losing it."

He looked at his hands, saw nothing remotely capable of this.

"I'll tend to Rachel," she said. "You just do what I was doing. Do you understand?"

He nodded, or something like it, began rubbing one of the cloths over his hands and forearms. *The plan, beat the plan.*

Rachel let out another scream, her voice ragged and getting worse. Claire relinquished her spot and Frank put his hands where hers had been, felt what she described, was aware of the effort she'd been expending to keep the cord free, his own hands all thumbs. And something else: the baby's head moving, nothing he'd felt before, he and Ginny childless. Followed by the rush of what was at stake.

Damn You, I'm a truck driver.

The spasm passed. He was conscious of Claire kneading her hands, shaking them, wiping her face on her sleeve. Saying she'd be right back and hurrying toward the kitchen.

There was a short sharp yell, the sound of falling. Heavily. Long seconds of nothing, then gasps. *Damnit,* the spilled water: He hadn't warned her.

"Are you all right?" he called.

More gasps. Rachel moaning softly.

"Claire?... Talk to me."

She came into view angled against the jamb, her face gray and hard set. Holding her wrist at an awkward angle, the knuckles on her clutching hand white with effort, her voice a whisper through bared teeth:

"Looks like you're it — Doctor."

Richard Barre

From four until dawn it was touch and go, everything going wrong that could, at several points Frank having to let go and rub feeling back into his own hands. Meanwhile, Claire did what she could with Rachel: comforting, coaching, using her good hand to wipe the girl's forehead and give her water. Gritting her own teeth. Directing Frank under her breath. Rachel exhausted beyond noticing, barely able to push when told.

In addition to the cord prolapse, the baby's shoulders wouldn't pass, Frank having to maneuver the slippery wedged form until he could grasp an arm, gently work it around and through. Not wanting to think about the last resort – almost certain they'd lose Rachel. Even money on the baby.

But then at dawn, light beginning to show at the windows, Rachel gave a final push and the baby simply fell into Frank's hands.

A boy.

With no face.

Frank's mouth opened in horror.

"Pay attention. That's the caul," Claire said, "the membrane. You have to remove it. NOW."

God almighty. "How do I – ?"

"You make a hole and lift it off. *Gently…*that's right."

The baby's face appeared; it gasped, took a breath, stopped, began turning blue.

"It's not breathing."

"Check it's mouth."

"Clear," he answered in a voice not sounding like his.

"Listen to me: You're going to have to give it air...puffs, Frank – yes. Wait. Okay, now some more..."

Come on, breathe.

"Again," she said.

Nothing.

"Another set."

Live, Frank thought, don't you dare crap out on me after all this. *"LIVE,"* he heard himself shouting. *"PLEASE."*

And at that, the baby began to breathe.

They sat on the floor with coffee he'd fixed after getting the generator going, nothing really wrong with it, the thing just old. As they sat, they listened to Rachel's deep breathing, watched the small form settle against her. *"Thank you, Doctor,"* she'd said to him as the baby

Richard Barre

nursed. *"Thank you."* Words that echoed as she and the baby lapsed into exhausted sleep.

Claire raised the wrist he'd wrapped for her. "Feels better, I think. Sure you're not a doctor?"

"Lord, I'm tired."

"Yeah," he agreed, although he was still wired from it, the feeling of the baby in his hands, suddenly aware of the day.

Happy Birthday, Ginny.

"Well, you did it," Claire said wearily.

"Showed *him*."

"Or did you?"

He smiled at having no ready answer, at the persistence he'd disliked in her about a thousand years ago. He noticed how the glow had returned to her face.

"At least admit it's food for thought," she said.

"Food for thought," he allowed.

He cut pie for them and they ate without speaking, Frank casting frequent glances at the baby. Not quite the first Christmas, but...

Claire finished hers, set her fork down. "They say

the caul brings luck. He'll never die by drowning."

"That's a relief."

She rubbed tired eyes. "Sometimes they have the phone lines fixed by daybreak."

He tried, and they did. He dialed his dispatcher first, then the highway patrol, saying he'd meet them at the wreckage and where they'd find it. As he was talking, pacing, he realized how much better his knee was, the limp close to gone. He walked over to Rachel and the baby; after a bit he was conscious of Claire beside him.

"Go ahead, hold him," she said.

"Rachel won't mind?"

"You're her doctor, remember?"

He picked up the baby in its blanket, felt it against him, this tight little ball of muscle. He smelled Rachel's milk, the light sweet fragrance of it. He felt things melting and sliding off.

Claire walked to the window. "Sun's out."

He joined her, all that white difficult to look directly into. "I should be going," he said. "While there's a break."

She went into the living quarters, came back with a plaid wool coat. "You're about Sewell's size. You're welcome to it." Handing it to him, taking the baby in return.

"Are you sure?"

"No one's worn it but him," she said. "I'm sure."

He put it on, felt its rough heft, looked at her nodding, the baby at her shoulder, a kind of radiance about them. "Since Ginny, I'm not very big on goodbyes."

"Since Sewell, neither am I." Taking the hand he offered. "You did fine in there, Frank. You know that, don't you?" Eyes scanning his face, as though trying to memorize it.

"Other way around."

"No. She made it because of you, let that in. Now go."

She opened the door and let him out, closed it quickly so as not to chill the baby. Frank stood on the porch. And suddenly the something that had been bothering him popped into his mind. He turned back, but the sun was bright on the windows, making it hard to see in.

"I never told you my last name." Raising his voice and squinting through the glass. "When you introduced me as Dr. Shane. How'd you know it was Shane?"

"I just knew," he heard her say.

"I don't – "

He couldn't see them at all then. Just the brightness.

"Happy Christmas, Frank. Have a good life."

He opened his eyes to piercing sun, a tapping at the window.

"You okay in there?"

With effort, Frank uncoiled from the position he'd stiffened into; he saw blue sky, endless snow, a salt-and-pepper CHP. Dark sunglasses, breath showing around his face.

"I said, are you okay?"

Frank rolled down his window to air like ice.

"I think so." Checking his watch: more than ten hours he'd been out. A snowplow clanked by on the highway. About the way he felt.

"Looks like you played a little crack-the-whip. Lucky you didn't end up in the river."

Frank touched his head where it hurt, a crust of dried blood.

"Lucky to be wearing that coat, too. Case you didn't notice, it got down to four degrees last night."

Frank felt the wool plaid, thick under his fingers.

"Can you start it up?"

Richard Barre

"What's that?"

"See if she'll run. You sure you're okay?"

Ignition. He reached for the keys, turned them, felt the engine catch, settle into idle.

The patrolman nodded.

"Thanks," Frank said.

"You need anything?"

"Not that comes to mind." Still trying to shake it off, figure out what the –

"Anytime you're ready, then."

The CHP wrote something in his notebook, stowed it, started crunching toward his car.

"Officer?" Frank called after him. "Excuse me. Are you familiar with the area?"

"I should be," he said, turning back. "Grew up in Dunsmuir down the road."

"The name Bethany ring a bell? Tiny place with a café?"

He puzzled on it. "No, I don't – wait a minute... right. Across the river?"

"That's the one," Frank said, glad for at least some frame of reference. Not everything, but a start.

"I doubt it," the CHP said. "Bethany got wiped off the map when their reservoir broke. Years ago. Saw pictures of it once. Nothing left but the foundations.

Frank just stared. "But it's there. I was there."

"Some other life, maybe. Water drowned everybody, except for a baby they found. A boy."

The caul. The caul brings luck.

"I remember my granddad talking about it. Kid grew up to be a doctor. Delivered lots of the locals back then."

He'll never die by drowning.

"Son, you sure you're all right?"

Frank nodded, though it took a second.

"I was you, I'd have that bump looked at when you hit a clear exit. Plows are doing what they can, but don't expect miracles."

"Say that again?"

"Just take it slow."

Frank watched him get into his unit, swing around after the snowplow, over a rise and gone. For a while he sat there, all of it washing over him. Then there was nothing left but to head out. He reached up and touched Ginny's picture, told her he loved her, not to worry about him anymore. That he'd be okay.

He'd put it in gear, was about to let out the clutch, when his gaze drifted again across the drop-off, to the river and the trees beyond. Even with the sun in his eyes, that had to be, *had to be*, a wisp of smoke curling up from where Bethany lay.

Two thousand hardcover copies of *Bethany* were printed by Capra Press. One hundred copies have been numbered and signed by the author and Mr. Crais. Twenty-six copies in slipcases were also lettered and signed by both.

About Capra Press

Capra Press was founded in 1969 by the late Noel Young. Among its authors have been Henry Miller, Ross Macdonald, Margaret Millar, Edward Abbey, Anais Nin, Raymond Carver, Ray Bradbury, and Lawrence Durrell. It is in this tradition that we present the new Capra: literary and mystery fiction, lifestyle and city books. Contact us. We welcome your comments.

815 De La Vina Street, Santa Barbara, CA 93101
805-892-2722 • www.caprapress.com